Beaser the Bear's
Rocky Mountain
Christmas

written by Patricia Derrick

illustrated by Doug Hoch

Dedication
This book is dedicated to my daughter Tricia Abbott.
In her eloquent way of speaking truths, Tricia explained how to
'grow your heart by sharing.'
These inspirational tidbits inspired my heart to write this book.

Animalations Publishing
Patricia Derrick
4186 Melodia Songo Court
Las Vegas, Nevada 89135
www.Animalations.com

ISBN: 978-1-933818-09-2

Author Copyright © 2007 by Patricia Derrick
Illustrations Copyright © 2007 Animalations
Music Copyright © 2007

All rights reserved, including the right of reproduction in whole or in part, in any form.

Printed in Korea.

Three R's Before Reading

Rhythm

Rhyme

Repetition

Three R's before Reading (**Rhythm, Rhyme and Repetition**) uses multi-sensory stimulation to fire neurons in the brain. Multi-sensory stimulation creates strong connections between neurons. With strong connections, learning becomes easier.

Rhythm is found in music and movement. Rhythm is experienced when we listen to musical sounds, decipher what is heard and move to the beat. Children will literally get up on their feet and start dancing when they hear "foot tapping" music. Children will want to participate when they hear rhythm. Participation can include everything that makes up a "multi-sensory" experience for the child.

Rhyme: Rhyming verses provide patterns. Patterns are found in poetry, rhyming books and in musical songs. Children love the sound of patterns. They can feel what they hear throughout their bodies. Patterns stimulate the right side of the brain. The right side of the brain is responsible for math and spatial relationships, as well as language.

Repetition: Children love to repeat stimulating experiences over and over again. When children ask to do an activity again, they are really saying, "I want to feel those sensations again." Children feel sensations when the activity is "multi-sensory". If a child is given an opportunity to participate in a multi-sensory book, the child will want to read that particular book over and over again.

Animalations books provide multi-sensory stimulation that makes learning easier for children.

Copyright 2006

Beaser the Bear headed home
To his tinsel covered den.
What a joy filled season this is,
With Christmas 'round the bend.

Beaser could see bear cubs
From the trail down the way.
They didn't have food or a family
Or a bear den where they could stay.

Beaser lives with Mrs. Beaser
In their Rocky Mountain den.
And along with their two bear cubs
A fine Christmas they will spend.

Beaser's cubs,
    Rickity and Snickity
Know that Santa
    brings them toys.
But Beaser wants
    his cubs to learn,
How to feel
    Christmas joy.

But Beaser needs time to think,
To find the words to say.
So for now Beaser tells his cubs,
"Hey, go outside and play."

Beaser sat down and thought
Of when he was a cub.
And how he couldn't wait for Christmas
To get his big pile of stuff.

Then Beaser also remembered,
It's not about the toys.
It's about sharing with others,
That will bring Christmas joys.

Because when you
share with others
You'll feel it
deep inside.
It will bring a smile
upon your face.
A smile you
cannot hide.

Beaser pondered
what his Papa said,
"**Grow your heart**
by sharing.
If you will give
to others,
You'll be filled with
Christmas caring."

Time passed by very quickly.
Bear cubs came home from play.
Beaser had a special message
He would share with them today.

For Rickity and Snickity,
Christmas joy they don't feel.
All they feel is what they want
And for now, they want their meal.

Beaser shared, while they ate,
The story of when he was small.
And how receiving a pile of stuff,
Really had no meaning at all.

Beaser told of opening stuff,
And when he was all through,
He had so much he could not use,
He wondered what he should do.

At that moment Beaser understood
What it was he should do.
Give his extra stuff to other cubs
And make their dreams come true.

Beaser told his little cubs,
"I never went without.
I simply gave away the things
I did not care about."

Sometimes these things were new.
Sometimes they were almost new.
Yet it really didn't matter much
To the cubs I gave them to.

Then he told Rickity and Snickity
Of the cubs down the way.
How they didn't have food or a family
Or a bear den where they could stay.

The cubs listened to their Papa.
Then they had something to say,
"Papa, let's not wait 'til Christmas.
Let's **grow our hearts** today!"

So Rickity and Snickity searched
In closets and cupboards, too.
They said, "Finding treasures to give awa
Is not so hard to do!"

But then something happened
That surprised Beaser that day.
His cubs said, "We have lots of room.
Can we invite those cubs to stay?"

Well sure enough
the homeless cubs
Came to Beaser's den
to stay.

Papa Beaser
was so proud,

He shed Beaser tears
that day.

Big Beaser tears fell to the earth
As he hugged his family tight.
Beaser's den was so filled with love
On that joy filled Christmas night.

So how can you feel Christmas joy?
By now I'm sure you know.
It's giving away your extra stuff,
That will make **your heart grow!**

Teacher Parent Activities

Beaser the Bear's Rocky Mountain Christmas provides opportunities for learning experiences beyond reading the book. Use the suggested activities on this page to provide age appropriate learning for all children participating in *Beaser the Bear's Rocky Mountain Christmas.*

Social:

Discuss with the children what Christmas means to them and what they like most about Christmas. Discuss how it makes them feel when they read the story and find out the cubs on the trail do not have a bear den or family to go home to. Discuss how they felt when Beaser's cubs invited the bear cubs to come home to stay with them.

Can you grow your heart by giving to others? Explain that growing your heart in this story has a figurative meaning. It means you can fill your heart with emotion and love for others and in doing so you can enrich your own life.

Encourage the children to visit a less fortunate family this weekend and share something with them. Then next week provide an opportunity for the children to explain their experience and how it made them feel.

As a family project, encourage children and parents to find items in their house that they can share with others. Provide opportunities for the children to explain how doing this can make the other family's dreams come true.

Music:

Encourage the children to participate in the music by singing and dancing. Children will hear the music and respond by dancing in their own unique way. Allow children to participate in the song as much as they desire. As the children become more familiar with the story, they will increase their participation.

Art:

Give the children an opportunity to draw a picture of the family they would like to share with. Remind them to show the expressions on the faces of the family members receiving the gifts.

Then provide an opportunity for the children to show the expressions on members of their own family as they share with others.

Give the children an opportunity to explain drawings to others in the group. Self esteem will "sizzle" as children show their work and explain how they plan to share with others this Christmas season. Invite children to read their work to family members, friends, and grandparents, as well as post their drawings on home refrigerators to share with others over and over.

Language:

Provide an opportunity for the following role-playing activity:

One group of children find extra "stuff" to give another family. The children explain each item as they find it. The group then role plays going to another family's house, knocking on the door and giving "stuff" to the children in the house. When they are all finished, members of each family (giving family and receiving family) explain how this activity made them feel.

Think of other activities to "grow your heart" during the Christmas season. How can you "grow your heart' all year long?

Science Notes:

Rocky Mountain bears spend almost half their lives in winter bear dens. They spend up to 5 months either inside or living near their bear den. Bears will either dig their den or use a hollow tree or cave. Bear dens sometimes have tunnels that open up into chambers. Bears line the chambers with grass or tree limbs.

Insulation during the winter is provided by snow that covers the den and the entrance to the den. Rocky Mountain bears hibernate in their dens and come out in the spring.

Bear cubs are born in the winter in the mother bear's den. Female bears usually have one to three cubs at a time. Bear cubs keep safe and warm in their mother bear's den.

Cubs live with their mother until they are two to three years old. By this time they have learned what to eat and how to find food on their own. At two or three they go off to find their own bear den.

Beaser the Bear

Tempo: 140

Lyrics: Patricia Derri
Music: Jay Rams
Lyrics and Music Copyright: Animalations Publishi

Verse 2
Beaser told his cubs of when he was a bear cub too.
He had so much he couldn't use he wondered what to do.
At that moment Beaser knew just what he should do.
Give his stuff to other cubs to make their dreams come true.
You can grow your heart in a very simple way.
Give away your extra stuff and start it today.

Verse 3
Beaser told his little cubs I never went without.
I simply gave away the things I did not care about.
Sometimes they were new or sometimes almost new.
Yet it didn't matter to the cubs I gave them to.
You can grow your heart in a very simple way.
Give away your extra stuff and start it today.

Verse 4
Search through your den for treasures hidden away.
But you don't need to wait for Christmas; you can start it toda
Then on Christmas morning with presents all around,
Deep inside a cub like you a big heart will be found.
You can grow your heart in a very simple way.
Give away your extra stuff and start it today.
Give away your extra stuff and start it today.

Patricia Derrick, Author

Master of Education: University of Utah.
Early Childhood and Elementary School Educator
Owner and Operator of Early Learning Schools: 30 years
Assistant Professor, Metropolitan State College, Mesa College Campus, GJ Colorado

Author Patricia Derrick is available for speaking engagements and conferences.
Email: info@animalations.com for more information

Doug Hoch has been illustrating for 25 years. His work has been collected internationally. He has conducted seminars at universities nationwide. Doug lives in Lowville, New York. When he is not illustrating children's books, he ventures out in the wilderness to paint landscapes.

Other Animalations Books
by Patricia Derrick

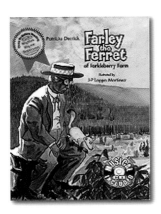

Farley the Ferret of Farkleberry Farm

When a drought threatens the boysenberry crop-which would mean no fresh jam and bread at the County Fair- area children respond to Farley's pleas for help.

Mr. Walrus and the Old School Bus

Mr. Walrus drives all the friends around town in the old school bus. They make many exciting stops along their way. But, they must hurry and not be late for their 5 o'clock date.

Dody the Dog has a Rainbow

As Dody the Dog finds his way back home, he looks for his rainbow. His rainbow gives him hope and inspiration as he travels. Dody learns a brighter tomorrow is coming.

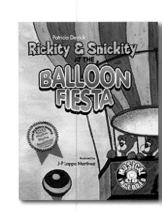

Rickity and Snickity

Two Rocky Mountain cubs sneak a ride in a Hot Air Balloon. Then they dream about doing it again next year. Will they be able to?

Riley the Rhinoceros

Riley the Rhinoceros gives rides to baby animals but he can't give rides to all the animals, because that would be pre-pos-ter-ous. Children will giggle as they imagine Riley giving rides to a giraffe, a python, and other jungle animals.

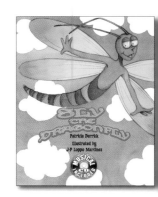

Sly the Dragonfly

Sly the Dragonfly loves to fly high. "I hear the wind whistling through my wings. It makes my heart wake up and sing". Sly encourages young readers to be the best that they can be.

Montgomery the Moose

With five distinct musical styles, Montgomery the Moose shakes his caboose for his friends. Young readers will learn to appreciate different kinds of music and participate in movement activities.

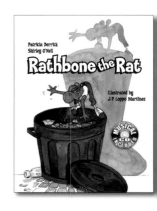

Rathbone the Rat

Rathbone the Rat is a mischievious rat. He travels through the town of Paris doing his mischievious deeds. Finally his friends help him and he learns a lesson.

Books available at your local book store, BarnesandNoble.com, Walmart.com, Amazon.com, selected Costco's and Sam's Clubs